Henrietta

there's no one better

Martine Murray

ALLEN&UNWIN

ACKNOWLEDGEMENTS

I would like to acknowledge the invaluable work of Verity Prideaux in the making of *Henrietta*. Thank you for a being patient and willing co-pilot in the design and layout of this book. Without you and your glorious patterns and textures, Henrietta would have had a very drab take-off.

First published in 2004
First paperback edition published in 2008

Allen & Unwin
83 Alexander St
Crows Nest NSW 2065
Australia
Phone: (61 2) 8425 0100
Fax: (61 2) 9906 2218
Email: info@allenandunwin.com
Web: www.allenandunwin.com

National Library of Australia
Cataloguing-in-Publication entry:
Murray, Martine, 1965 –
Henrietta : there's no one better.
ISBN 978 1 74114 718 6.
1. Imagination in children – Juvenile fiction.
I. Title.
A823.4

Cover and text design by Martine Murray and Verity Prideaux
Typeset in 13 pt Sabon by Verity Prideaux
Printed in China by Everbest Printing Co. Ltd.

3 5 7 9 10 8 6 4 2

Henrietta P. Hoppenbeek
would like this book to be dedicated to the
Wonderful Witches of Westgarth,
Nessie Noo, Cal E. Wag and Emsie T.

And also to Squeezy and Clare Bear,
and to Clive and Pete and Hobbit,
and Nigelo and Rico and Broni and Soni
and Beast
and the the faraway but ever near Jennie Higgie.

But that seems like a lot of people,
so instead this book is dedicated to
the friends you have lived with
and the family they are to you.

Henrietta P. Hoppenbeek the first

Allow me to introduce myself properly.
I am Henrietta P. Hoppenbeek the First, future Queen
of the Wide Wide Long Cool Coast of the Lost Socks,
and the only person in the even Wider World to have
visited the Island of the Rietta.

Don't forget that, because when I do become Queen, you may just want to ask me for a sunny part of the kingdom to lie about in with your dog. You never know.

Anyone who knows me well can call me Henri. But only if you know me really well, and not if you pull my hair like Bartley Baker does.

I'm a good wiggler, and sometimes

I'm *exhillperating* and sometimes I'm *expasperating*

I have a brother called Albert,
but he's only the size of a sock.

Not really.
He's probably about the same size
as a sewing machine,
only he can't sew.

a not-at-all,
not-one-bit
best friend
called Bartley
Baker

I have a mad brown dog called Madge,

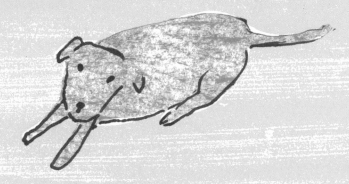

two white mice called Flora and Dora,

a best friend called Olive Higgie,
hair like spaghetti,
a diamond crown,
a woolly mammoth,
long green socks
and a big bad habit of making things up.

(I don't really have a woolly mammoth.)

It's only Madge wearing a woolly mammoth coat

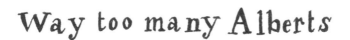

Way too many Alberts

Luckily, there's only one Albert in our family.
If there were more than one,
that would be way too many Alberts.
Can you imagine a whole house full of Alberts?

Alberts on the bookshelf,

Alberts in the washing machine,

Alberts in the shoe cupboard,

Alberts in the sink,

Alberts
in the lounge room,
slouching on the couch,

Alberts in the veggie patch,
crouching on the cabbage,

Alberts on the tellie and Alberts on the phone,

Alberts under my feet and Alberts on my nerves.

Oh boy, in a house full of Alberts there'd be a whole lot of howling and sleeping and burping and not many chocolate ripple cakes getting cooked and nothing being invented.

That's why it's lucky I'm here.
To make sure things keep happening.
Like when Mum is trying to put Albert to sleep,
I play the drums in the kitchen.
When I bang the end of the wooden spoon
on the wok it sounds like cracking thunder
and it makes my mum come running
with her face all screwed up, making

shhhhh shhhhh

noises, which go quite well with the drums.

She says, Henrietta, you're exasperating!

It's because I'm better at drumming than she is.
Mum only knows how to make *shhhh* noises.
Dad sometimes plays guitar,
but Mum says he only knows three songs
and she's sick of them.

Here's what I can do

on the way to Africa

I can ride the chair to Africa.
Or I can become a very
astounding statue.
I can become a duelling rhinoceros,
a surf champion,
a prehistoric tortoise,
an acrobat, a bushranger
or a high-and-mighty lady
singing hallelujah,
praise the land of agreeable chairs.
I can keep a secret,
I can make my dad's undies
into an absolutely superb hat,
I can play chair guitar and
then I can slam all the doors
in the whole house
before you can say,
'Oh my Lord, Henrietta,
do you have to make such a racket?'
I can lean back and let it all come easy.

surf champion

duelling rhinocero

prehistoric tortois

acrob

high-and-mighty lady

keeping a secret

superb hat

bushranger

"bang"

letting it all come easy

chair guitar

reaching for the biscuit tin

I reckon I could even convince
a woolly mammoth to shampoo his hair.
Don't worry, when Albert is old enough
I'll teach him everything I know,
except how to reach the biscuit tin.

I can't really keep a secret.

Here's what I want to be

Not a king, because kings can't fart. And not a soldier, because they have to take orders and walk all stiff.

And not a mother, because they have to clean up.

yuk

And not a dad, because they have to clean up, too.

And especially not a dentist, because if you were a dentist no one would want to come and see you. Not unless they had a toothache. What kind of guest is that? Not a fun one, I can tell you.

Maybe I would like to be a cloud,
but I can't be sure.
I know I would like to be superb,
like Uncle George's new car,

and occasionally a **genius**,

but not so much
that the world
would depend on me
to invent something
in a crisis.

What I really want to be is an explorer.

Explorification

I practise every day.
What I like doing best is walking BIG steps
without looking.

I always leave a trail behind me.

Just in case.

But it's best before dinner time,
when I get in the bath
and sail the bathtub
to undiscovered lands
without snakes.

Sometimes I take Albert,
and I head straight for the
Land of One Thousand Alberts,
where I drop him off for a long holiday.
In the Land of One Thousand Alberts
they all hang upside-down in trees
and close their eyes and wear snorkels
so you can't hear them howling.

You can only hear very superb songs sung
by a host of invisible lady singers from Budapest.
Then I look out for the
Wide Wide Long Cool Coast of the Lost Socks.

It's lucky Mum doesn't come with me,
because she would definitely bring
all the lost socks home
and put them back into pairs.
But me, I just wave and wiggle
at the naughty escaper socks
and leave them to be individuals
under the palm trees.

On my way,
I sail past a Pelican
standing on a rock.
The Pelican is wearing a red raincoat
and he flaps his wings every now and then,
just to make sure you don't mistake him
for a very small lighthouse
or a mushroom.
He can't open his beak, though,
because he has something
inside.

I know what it is.

A **naughty** word.
Like what Dad says
when Madge takes his shoe
and gives it a good chew
in the back garden
and leaves it there,
lost and wet and squashed
and covered in dog slobber.

Meet the Rietta

By far the best land I go to
is the Island of the Rietta.
I bet you've never even heard of a Rietta.
In fact, I might be the only single person
who has ever seen one.
That's because I have a special relationship
with the Rietta.
See, I'm Henrietta,
that's half a Hen and half a Rietta.

Everyone knows what hens are,
because they squawk a lot and carry on,
but no one has ever seen a Rietta.
No one except me, of course.

A Rietta isn't quite an animal and it isn't
quite a person and it isn't quite a piece of furniture
or an antique car, either,
in case you were thinking it might be.
A grown-up Rietta has big blotchy spots,
but a baby one has small dotty dots.
A Rietta only eats chocolate ripple biscuits.
It never eats brussel sprouts, never.
And it likes to wear a cake tin on its head,
in case a chocolate ripple cake
should fall from the sky.
A Rietta gets sad if you leave it alone
or say mean things to it. On the other hand,
if you play with a Rietta for a while
its naughty nature rubs off on you
and you end up doing naughty things,
like jumping on the bed and making a hullabaloo.
A Rietta tends to be confused and sometimes lonely,
but it always makes the best of things.
So, if you see one,
be sure to say something encouraging like...

Oh, what spectacular

spots you have!

And also be sure to play with it,
because all Riettas like to play.

When I park my bath,
the Rietta trots up and looks inside,
because Riettas always hope for presents.
They can't help it. I always bring a pillow,
and the Rietta eats a hole in the pillow and throws
all the feathers in the air and starts to laugh.
It doesn't squawk, it makes oink noises like a pig.
Then it gets tired and lies down
and expects me to tickle its tummy with a feather,
just like Mum sometimes does to me
when I'm going to sleep.
I don't drum for the sleeping Rietta,
I sing Rock My Soul, and the Rietta smiles
and hoots every now and then in appreciation.
Then I row my bath back to the bathroom where
Mum is always waiting with a big furry towel.
Don't worry, on the way I go to the
Land of One Thousand upside-down Alberts
and pick up our Albert,
because Mum would be mad if I left him
hanging in the tree.

Tickling Albert

I am standing by the heater in the nuddy.
I'm getting dry before I pop on my pyjamas,
of course.
And all of a sudden
I hear that Pelican on the rock,
opening his beak
and letting out
that word.

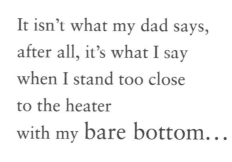

It isn't what my dad says,
after all, it's what I say
when I stand too close
to the heater
with my bare bottom...

sheezama

geeza

At bedtime
I give Albert a little friendly tickle,
to see if he hoots like the Rietta.
But he doesn't hoot, he just gurgles.

One day I might even take him with me,
when he's old enough.
We might just discover another land together.
Possibly the Land of the Grumpy Potatoes,
where I will lie down and some stray feathers
from the Island of the Rietta will fall from the sky
and land very softly on my eyelids,
so softly I can hardly even feel them...

List of Undiscovered Lands

Land of squashy and spiky things
Land of the fat Wombat called Graham
Land made of bird pooh
Land where only very rude people live
Land ruled by a LARGE old sunburnt Nose
Land where legs get lazy
Land that feels like a bean bag
Land where nothing adds up
Land of larger-than-you-can-ever-imagine
Land of the grumpy potatoes and the half-hearted
army of brussel sprouts

My dad's like my dog

Dad's alarm wakes me up. It doesn't wake Dad up,
even though it beeps right next to his ear.
I think his ear is getting tired of hearing.
Mum elbows him in his side,
but he just snorts because he's used to that.

So I let Madge in, and we jump on the bed
and Madge licks Dad on the face,
and that usually wakes him up.
Madge is brown all over except for her tongue,
which is pink. My dad isn't brown all over,
and his name isn't Madge,
but in some particular ways he's just like Madge.
(Don't tell him I said that.)

Dad

madge

For one thing, both Madge and Dad have an office.
Dad's office is in the city,
Madge's office is in the backyard.

Dad's office is a room with a desk and a computer
and some empty old coffee cups.

Madge's office is that squashed
patch of grass under the tree
which is covered in rotten
stinky bones and old cans
and bits of hose.

Mainly what Madge does
in her office is chew stuff,
especially if it looks
threatening,
like a hose.

Mainly what Dad does
in his office is read stuff,
especially if it's about golf.

Once, it was Dad's birthday,
but no one remembered.

Not even Dad.

He went to his office,
because somebody's got to earn a crust,
and Mum went into the garage
to make bowls out of clay, because she's an artist,
and Albert had a nap, because he's a baby,
and I made a cushion castle,
because I'm an inventor.

But then Madge got bored,
because she's a crazy brown dog
who needs a lot of patting,
so she went to work in her office,
and I definitely had to help her,
because someone has to make sure
things around here get done
properly.

First, she got a cushion off the couch
and then she dragged it out to her office,
where she pretended it was a wild animal.
She got it in her mouth
and she shook it and leapt around
as if the cushion was attacking her.
It was just like what Dad does with a cushion
when he's watching the footy on tellie,
especially when the Tigers are losing.

When Madge had triumphed over the cushion,
she chewed it up
and left white bits of stuffing
all over her office,
and it looked like it had been snowing.

Then Madge and I both caught a whiff of something in the air...

Mum was cooking, and thank my *lucky*

and doubly thank my *lucky star*

No, it was a much MUCH

It was the best thing possible, a thing that make

chocolate

I ran inside. First I said, *ripper*

can I lick the bowl? and then, lastly

It was a birthday

tars above, it wasn't kidney bean stew

bove, it wasn't even brussel sprouts.

ore thrilling thing.

iettas very, very excited. You guessed it:

ripple cake

hen I said, what's going on?

aid, please, which always ups your chances.

ake for Dad.

Then Mum saw the remains of the cushion
in Madge's office, and I was glad it was Madge
who did it and not me because Mum wasn't happy,
I can tell you.
Madge was heading for a whopping big smack,
but luckily for Madge there's one whiff on the air
that's even better than chocolate,
and that's rubbish.

Madge always runs away
on rubbish day.
She can't help herself.
She jumps the fence
and scurries off
to roam the streets
and plunder bins
and roll in the stinkiest stuff
she can find.

Albert had banana and gurgled on the floor

We all waited for Madge and Dad
to come home.

Mum sat cross-legged and said,

Omm

It calms her down.

I watched tellie. It calms me down.

We waited and we waited...
Mum said she was getting a headache.
I said I was getting a bellyache.
(That's the pain you get when you can smell
chocolate cake but you're not supposed to eat it.)

Where was Dad?

And more importantly,
was that chocolate cake feeling lonely and unloved
sitting all alone in the kitchen
while Mum had her eyes closed?

And where was Madge?

Definitely more importantly,
did it need me to show it some love?

Dad got home first.

He was singing Happy Birthday to himself.

Mum wouldn't kiss him because he smelt like a pub.

Then Madge came home.

Mum told Madge to go outside because she stunk
of rubbish and she'd destroyed a cushion.

I said, 'Happy Birthday, Dad,'
and he gave me a kiss, even though he was smelly.

Then Mum went to get the cake.

It had disappeared.

Right off the kitchen table.

poof

Just like that. Gone!

Where do you think it had gone? I'll tell you.

First it went into Madge's office.

And then it went into Madge's stomach.

That's the other thing Dad and Madge
have in common: they both can't resist chocolate.

Only Madge doesn't get a tummy bulging
over her pants, like Dad does.

But then Madge doesn't wear pants.

When they're in trouble,
Dad and Madge sit on the verandah.
But when they're out of trouble
there's one place they both like to be.

On the couch.

Lucky it's a big couch.

How to become an animal

Okay, there are two rules:

1. Best time to become
   an animal is on weekends

2. But don't do it
   if your dad has a headache
   or if Albert is sleeping

While it's easier to become an animal
than it is to become an astronaut,
let me tell you, it's not as simple as hiding
a green pea in your nostril…

First of all, you definitely must get dirty.

If you want
to become an animal
you can't worry
about getting
mud on your knees,

or leaves that
stickers to your knickers,

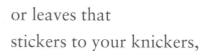

or wet on your bum,

or knots in your hair.

That's all part of the job.

Second of all, for no apparent reason you can howl.
Especially if the world seems contradictory...
if it's raining just when you want to go outside.
I open my heart and howl,
and Albert sometimes joins in, and Mum says,

Oh my Lord, must you?

So I dash upstairs and get glamorous instead.
And, when I'm supposed to eat
brussel sprouts or kidney bean stew,
I give it a reluctant sniff and turn up my nose.
And when I eat ice-cream,
I'm a much MUCH nicer animal.
And, sometimes, just sometimes, after lunch,
just because Albert has to snooze,
I come across a small moment of idleness.

But afterwards, look out!

The sun is shining again
and I'm getting all wriggly and jumpy.

What I imagine is, if I run fast enough up the

I might just take off

road and down the green hill,

And then again, I might not.

It doesn't matter.
If the sky is blue enough,
I absolutely
must sing about it
anyway.

Here's what I sing:
'Well, I'm Henrietta
and I've got long green socks with toes
and a little brother called Albert
who only knows one word

fish'

And when I'm very pleased with myself,

I dance like a wild thing.

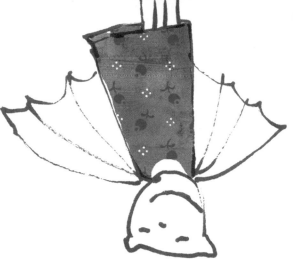

And if I can't think
of what else to do,
I simply
astonish myself.
I turn the world up
the other way.

At the end of the day, when my tummy is rumbling,
I go inside and purr at Mum,
who is making spaghetti for dinner.
She says,

Henrietta,
no sticking peas up your nostrils and
no writing rude words with the spaghetti

But I'm too hungry
to think about
hiding peas
or writing

Sheezdmageeza

63

Oh Lordy Lordy,
I'm as hungry
as a bungry,
and don't ask me
what a bungry is
because that's
another story.

Flora and Dora

In my bedroom,
not far from my bed,
just sitting on top of
the broken-down record player,
is
a wooden box
with a glass window
at the front.

In the box is Flora

and also Dora

You can't really tell who is Flora and who is Dora,
because they both have exactly the same
twitchy expression on their faces,
though I think Flora is just a little bit fatter.
(And a little bit foxier, too.)

What Flora and Dora like to do best of all
is to run very fast round and round inside a wheel.
Only for fun, though. Not like my dad who also
runs round and round in a circle as fast as he can,
(which isn't that fast).
Then he puffs.
You never hear Flora or Dora puff.
You only hear them squeaking on about
mouse things,
like pizza crumbs and how to hide in a toaster
if you see a cat.

Flora and Dora are very best friends.
Like me and my friend, Olive Higgie.
But you can easily tell the difference
between me and Olive Higgie
because she has black hair and she likes pickles,
but I don't.
Also, I can stand on my head and she can't,
but she can play chopsticks on the piano.
Neither of us squeaks much,
unless someone tickles us.

One day, Olive Higgie comes over
to eat Cheezles and play.
We put the Cheezles on our fingers
and then we start throwing socks, and Olive Higgie,
who is trying to stand on her head,
accidentally bumps into the chair
and the chair accidentally falls over
and accidentally crashes into the box
on top of the broken-down record player
where Flora and Dora quite purposefully live.

OOPS says Olive Higgie,

and she puts her hand over her mouth.

Uh oh I say,

because there's a big hole in the glass.

The next day, Flora is gone.
She must have crawled out the hole,
looking for pizza crumbs or bits of cheesecake.
Or maybe she wanted to see the sleepy green field
where you can run round in big circles.
I look for her everywhere,
even inside Dad's woolly socks,
and behind the stove
where lots of old bits of spaghetti go.
But she isn't anywhere.

My dad fixes the hole so that Dora won't go.
But I am worried. I know it will be lonely for Dora
without her best friend Flora there.
Dora will have no one to share
special kinds of crumbs with.
No one to watch her run round the wheel
like a mighty champion.

Dad says,

Don't worry, mice don't get lonely

Olive Higgie and I take it in turns to hold Dora
very softly in the palms of our hands,
so she won't feel alone.
Dora stops running round in her wheel.
I guess she just doesn't feel like it any more.

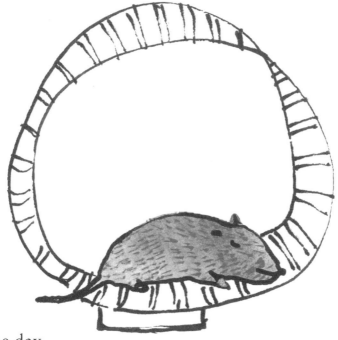

One day,
I find Dora lying completely still in the wheel.
I can tell she has died because of the way she looks.

'See,' I say to my dad. 'Dora has died of loneliness.'
And now he believes me that all things get lonely.

Even ants and beetles and cockroaches get lonely.

Even turtles, even squids and even sardines.

and my mum said especially doves, because they fall in love,

and especially dogs, like our dog Madge,

who always wants me to scratch her tummy.

Olive Higgie and I bury Dora near the daffodils,
and then we hold hands and close our eyes
and think good thoughts about Dora.

Olive Higgie says
she saw Flora sitting there, too,
but I'm not sure she really did.

The terrible terrible earthquake

One day, Olive Higgie says to me
that she has an Iggie in her bedroom.
And I say, 'What's an Iggie?'
And she says, 'An Iggie is a very good friend
of the Rietta who used to live on the Isle of Iggie,
but now lives with me because there was a terrible,
terrible earthquake on the Isle of Iggie.'
I say, 'Sheezamageeza!
A terrible earthquake on the Isle of Iggie.'
Then I say, 'What does an Iggie look like?'
And she does this drawing of an Iggie to show me,
and I say, 'That looks like a bandicoot.'
So she draws it again and I'm pleased to see
it doesn't have spots, since no one likes a copy cat.

And I say, 'What does an Iggie eat?'
And she says, 'Pickles and Cheezles.'
And I say, 'Oh my Lordy Lordy, pickles.'
I mean, who can seriously stomach pickles?
That poor old Iggie.
But Olive Higgie isn't worried. She says,
'Well, maybe the Rietta would like to meet the Iggie.'

And I say, 'Hmmm, yes, I think the Rietta would.'

So, next time I get in my bath
I speed off to the Island of the Rietta
and I go directly right past the
Wide Wide Long Cool Coast of the Lost Socks,

not even checking to see if either of my
long red socks with toes was having a visit,
and when I get to the island,
I am sorry to say
that things aren't in a good state there.
Oh Lordy Lordy, no they aren't.

For a start, the island has changed colour.
It isn't green any more, it's brown.
It looks like a bit of mud.
I fear that there's been a terrible terrible earthquake.
But that isn't what has happened.

'Good grief. You won't believe it,'
calls out the Puffed-up Pelican,
who knows everything and likes to gossip.
'What a disaster!'
'What happened?' I say.

'Good grief. You won't believe it,' says the Pelican,
who can be repetitive when he's in the mood
for spreading disaster stories.

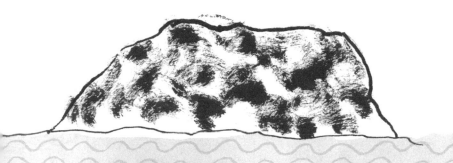

'Oh please,
go ahead and tell me
what happened,' I say.
And the Pelican sighs,
'Well, if you must know,
the trees were all cut down.
Imagine!'
'Sheezamageeza!' I say.
'No trees!
Lordy Lordy, what a disaster.'

The Rietta is lying next to a rock.
It doesn't hoot.
It hardly raises its head.

A Rietta can't live without trees,
so I absolutely have to save it.
I rub its ears, like I do to Madge,
and then I take it to my bathtub,
and together we sail home.

On the way
the Rietta
eats the soap,
and bubbles
come out
its mouth.

I wrap the Rietta in a towel,
just like my mum does to me.
Then I give it some ice-cream. It hoots with joy.
All Riettas hoot when they're happy.

It likes to sleep in my bed, but it snores...

and its spots rub off on the sheets.

Sometimes we creep into the kitchen,
while Mum is putting Albert to bed,
and we eat a little more ice-cream
straight from the tub.

It's the Rietta's
naughty nature
that makes me do it.

ice-cream

Other times, the Rietta looks out the window.
It just sits there and stares out
as if it has lost something in the night.
And that gets me thinking
about all the other lands out there,
because we need to find another land for the Rietta.
Like the

Land of the great untouched chocolate ripple

I tell the Rietta not to worry or feel sad,
because once it's bath time
we're going to do some more explorification.
We'll even take Albert with us,
because we could use an anchor man
and Albert is just the right size (sewing machine size)
to be an anchor,
just in case we need to stop and visit the Iggie
or rescue another Rietta,
because you just never know what will happen
once we get in that bath.

You never know!

Well, I'm Henrietta and
little brother who only know
cleverer than Albert, my socks ar
know what stars ✿ are made of
fed up, Albert's getting mucked
with honey on my tummy
in a muddle, my socks wit
I like my long green socks wit
So I know what, I'll whip
not the lot? Forget th
It's really not so rude
and gets a towel, says
a flibberty
I say, it's true
be one too
socks
nc

've got long green socks with toes and a
one word. fish. 🐟 I'm much older and
much longer and my favourite colour's red. I
nd I don't want to go to bed. Mum's getting
up, but I'm a grubby little sluggy 🐌
m hoppy like a mossie ✶ and my mind's
skew-whiff and my foot's 👟 in a puddle.
-oes, I don't want to get them wet.
them off! It's getting hot, ☀ why
frippery, I'll skin dippery!
to frolic in the nude. Mum sighs
not to fidget, 'must you be
gibbet?' I'm afraid I must,
and when Albert grows up, he'll
ill give him my long green
so he can do the 🧦🧦
frock-rocks